THE STUFFED ANIMAL

A CHRISTMAS STORY

JOHN DONALD O'SHEA

For information, or to order additional copies, please contact:

Fox and Hound Books
A Beacon Publishing Group Imprint
P.O. Box 41573 Charleston, S.C. 29423
800.817.8480 | foxandhoundbooks.com

Publisher's catalog available by request.

ISBN-13: 978-1-949472-36-3

ISBN-10: 1-949472-36-3

Published in 2021. New York, NY 10001.

First Edition. Printed in the USA.

My "Thank You"

First, I would like to thank my illustrator Jasmine Smith for doing what I couldn't do —illustrating my book. Next I wish to thank Cindy B. for telling me the story of her doll, Sabrina Ballerina. And most of all, I would like to thank my daughter, Erin O'Shea, for letting me be a part of her life and friendship with "Bunny" when she was a little girl, and for proofing and re-proofing my manuscript, and making many valuable suggestions to improve it.

Once upon a time, in a small town not far from here, there was a small shop called *The Stuffed Animal.* The proprietor was a middle-aged lady named Abigail Grace. She lived alone with her big, furry dog, "Furf"—which was short for "Fur Face." Those people who knew her well, and not many did, said she had but one abiding interest in life: Every Friday morning, no matter how inclement the weather, she could be found prowling the neighborhood garage sales. There, she would search for stuffed animals and dolls—not new ones, not beautiful ones, but shabby old teddies with their ears bitten off, and dolls who had lost their limbs. She would buy them for a nickel, a dime, or a quarter, and take them away.

Her neighbors said she put them in her shop, but they really didn't know because her shop was never open for business. But because they saw her carry boxes and bags into the shop and come out empty handed, that was their best guess. Especially since she called her little shop *The Stuffed Animal.* Perhaps because Miss Grace was such a private person who always kept to herself, the people of the small Victorian town never questioned her about her activities—that is, until Cindy Kim saw Miss Grace walking Furf, just after dark, one Christmas Eve.

Cindy crossed the street, and as Miss Grace neared the streetlamp just outside her shop, Cindy said, "Merry Christmas, Miss Grace." As she did, Furf gave Cindy his standard sniff-over and decided she meant his mistress no harm. "Merry Christmas to you, Cindy," replied the older lady.

"Miss Grace, there's something I've been meaning to ask you for a very long time ...."

"Yes, dear?"

"Miss Grace, do you remember, about ten years ago, coming to a yard sale at our house?"

"You say it was about 10 years ago?"

"Yes, ma'am. It was a hot summer day. You bought an old doll for a dime."

"Was she," asked Miss Grace, "a ballerina?"

"Yes, a lovely ballerina with beautiful golden hair and a green satin dress."

"No, dear. The doll I bought was missing both her dress and her head."

"Do you still have her? If you do," said Cindy, "I'd like to buy her back...."

"Whatever for?"

"I still miss her. She was my favorite doll."

As she spoke, the warm glow from the Victorian-style streetlamp illuminated Cindy's face. And for the next few minutes, as she told her story, her already soft face shone with the innocence of childhood. "I first saw her one steamy August day, when I was three, down at the Ben Franklin Store. She was in a large box, sitting on the top shelf along the left wall as one came in. The very first moment I saw her, I wanted her. I asked Mom to buy her, but she said it wasn't my birthday, and that we couldn't afford her. I think I stopped at the Ben Franklin every day for the next two months.

"Then one day, she was gone.... I cried my eyes out. But then after a week or so, I forgot her.

"Then, Christmas Eve came. We were poor in those days, and my sisters and I only got one present each. To make Christmas seem longer, I opened my present last. When I tore off the paper, there she was with her beautiful golden hair and lovely green ballerina dress. I called her Sabrina.

"When Mom, Dad, and my sisters were done opening their presents, they went to the dining room for dessert, but I stayed in the living room alone with Sabrina. The room was dark, except for the colored lights on the tree. I can still remember sitting in Dad's big stuffed chair and taking Sabrina into my arms for the first time.

"For the next two years, I took her everywhere with me. Then one day, as I was walking to my friend's house, a big dog ran up and grabbed Sabrina out of my arms and ran away. I chased him and eventually found Sabrina, but her head was gone, and so was her dress." And then, with just the hint of a tear in her eyes, Cindy finished her story.

"Later that summer, Mom put her in the yard sale without telling me. When I asked Mom where Sabrina was, she told me she had sold her and that you had bought her."

"She was your favorite doll?" Miss Grace asked, with the gentleness of one who truly understood.

"Oh yes, my most favorite, ever."

"I rather thought so...Why don't you come into my shop with me? We'll see if we can find her."

"Do you have many dolls for sale in your store?" asked Cindy.

The Stuffed Animal is not a store, my dear. It's .... well, it's rather a retirement home for dolls and teddies that were once the favorite toy of a small boy or girl."

"How do you know when a toy was a favorite toy?" asked Cindy.

"Oh, that's very easy," said Miss Grace, as she opened her purse, found her key, and opened the door of the shop. "Come in, it will be warmer in here."

As Cindy followed Miss Grace and Furf up the single step and into the shop, she noticed that the small front room which they had entered was softly lit by a small, blue-green, Tiffany-style table lamp.

The room had been decorated for Christmas. The most notable decoration was a rather large crèche, set against a backdrop of evergreen branches. The blue Christmas lights that illuminated the crèche, brought to mind the serenity and peace suggested by the familiar carol, "O Little Town of Bethlehem."

From the next room, Cindy could hear voices softly singing a Christmas carol, which she did not know. As she stood admiring the crèche, she said to Miss Grace, "I hear people caroling." Furf, in the meantime, laid down near the front door, as dogs do, and took a nap.

"Yes, it's Christmas Eve," replied Miss Grace.

As she looked back up, Cindy thought she saw something move in the shadow behind Miss Grace. At first, Cindy thought it might be an angora cat. Then, as she looked closer, she noticed a small toy soldier approach them. He wore a furry, black, beefeater's hat, a red tunic, and navy pants with a gold stripe. He looked, for all the world, like a Christmas Nutcracker.

"Merry Christmas, Miss Grace," said the toy soldier.

"Merry Christmas to you, Tommy," said Miss Grace.

"Miss Grace," said Cindy in amazement, "the toy soldier talked to you."

"Of course," said Miss Grace as if nothing unusual had happened. "Don't you remember Sabrina talking to you?"

Cindy paused and thought for a moment. "I'm not sure .... It was so long ago."

"At night, when your Mother tucked you in, and when you told Sabrina good night, can't you recall her saying 'night, night' to you? And when you took her in your arms and told her you loved her, didn't she snuggle right in and couldn't you hear her say 'I love you, too, Cindy?'" the older woman asked.

"We never said it very loud," interjected Tommy, "but we always said it. That's why we were your favorite toys. Dolls that don't talk to their friends never become a child's favorite toy and spend their entire lives on shelves or in a toy chest."

"Were you a little girl's favorite toy, too?" asked Cindy.

"Certainly not," said the little soldier in a voice that showed some degree of pique. "I had a little boy named Brian O'Malley. We met on his first birthday. I was a present from his Mother. His Dad was in the army, and his Mom wanted Brian to have a toy that reminded him of his father."

"Tommy was the first doll I found," said Miss Grace.

"He was my best friend," explained the little soldier. "I went everywhere with him. We played *cops and robbers* and *cowboys and Indians* together. He had a great imagination. I really liked it when we played the *Lone Ranger* and had to track down the Cavendish gang. That was neat."

"Then, when he started playing baseball, he took me to all of his games."

"How did you get here?" asked Cindy.

"Brian," Tommy said, "had taken me along to his baseball game. It was a big game. Brian's team won when he hit a homer in the ninth inning. When the game was over, in all the excitement, he left me in the dugout. I waited for him all night. It was the first time in years that we had not spent the night together.

"In the morning, a big red-headed boy with a crew cut found me there. He picked me up and tossed me into the weeds. I never saw Brian again. I always wondered if he came back for me. If he did, he didn't find me."

Miss Grace finished Tommy's story. "I was walking my dog, and Furf found him. His foot was sticking up. He was caught on the cane of a raspberry bush. I knew right away that he had been special to some child, so I decided to take him home, fix him up, and then try to locate his owner. I made him a new left arm to replace the one that had been ripped off. Then, I sewed on a new eye and gave him a new set of clothes."

"She's a very good doctor," said Tommy, enthusiastically. "All the dolls say so."

"Why didn't you tell her about Brian?" asked Cindy.

"I couldn't," Tommy replied. "She wasn't my best friend; she wasn't Brian...." Then with childlike sincerity, he asked, "To whom do you belong?"

"Pardon me?" asked Cindy, not quite understanding.

"Just as Sabrina was your doll, you were her little girl," explained Miss Grace. He's asking, "who your doll was?"

Cindy smiled. "My doll was Sabrina."

"I just saw her," said Tommy. "She was with the 'Christmas Dolls.' "

Miss Grace explained that the "Christmas Dolls" were the dolls who had been Christmas presents. As she did, a small brown teddy bear, with a tiny black nose, entered the room. The little bear was wearing a lovely red Christmas bow.

"Merry Christmas, everybody," said the furry little creature.

"That teddy bear is talking!" exclaimed Cindy.

"Sure, children love us teddies just as much as dolls."

"What's your name?" asked Cindy.

"I'm Susie," replied the little bear.

Cindy took a couple steps, bent over, and picked up the little bear. "Your fur is very soft. You're a beautiful little bear."

Susie chuckled, "You should have seen me when I first got here."

"When Susie first arrived, she was a very bare teddy bear," Miss Grace smiled.

"Donnie had hugged all my fur off," the bear explained.

"He'd also chewed off your nose and one ear," said Tommy.

"When I first found him, he was a sorry sight, indeed," said Miss Grace.

"Well, you're very beautiful now," said Cindy.

Tommy looked up at Miss Grace and said, "I told you; she's a very good doctor."

"Besides being a 'retirement home'," Susie offered, *The Stuffed Animal* is a wonderful animal hospital."

"Do you remember your little boy?" asked Cindy. "I think you called him Donnie?"

"Sure," said the bear. "Stuffed animals never forget."

Then the little bear recounted the story of how she had met Donnie.

"Donnie's Dad was a traveling salesman, who sold toys throughout the states of Illinois and Indiana. His dad saw me in a drug store in Terre Haute, and took me home.

Donnie was an only child, and he and I became great friends. I liked it best when it thundered and lightninged at night. We'd hide together under the covers, and Donnie's cocker spaniel would crawl in, too. He was soft like me, but he was really afraid of the thunder. Donnie's mother was nice, but I don't think she liked me."

"Why not?" asked Cindy.

And then with all the earnestness that only a stuffed animal can show, Susie said, "One day, while Donnie was taking his nap, she threw me down the garbage chute of the apartment building."

"You poor thing. The smell must have been awful," said Cindy.

"I couldn't smell a thing. By then, Donnie had bitten off my nose," said the little bear. "But I didn't like the dark."

"How did you rescue Susie from there?" Cindy asked Miss Grace.

"She didn't," said the teddy bear. "I found out later, that when Donnie woke up and discovered that I was gone, he cried so hard that his mother had to go down and get me. But then she tried to drown me! I got soap in my eyes and left ear. He had bitten off the other one. Finally, when I dried out, she let me have Donnie back."

"Then where did you find Susie?" Cindy asked again.

"For the next few months," said Susie, "Donnie and I were inseparable. But then, I saw less and less of him. And by the time he became three, I didn't see him anymore. Then one day, after I had not seen him for a long while, his mother came and got me, and put me out on the curb with the trash."

"That's awful!" Cindy could feel the teddy's loss as she imagined Susie sitting atop the contents of a garbage can. "What a way to treat a friend!" she said.

"I found Susie," said Miss Grace, "a little later that morning—again, while I was walking my dog. Furf is a terrific sniffer. I brought her here, made her a new fur coat, and stitched on a new ear and nose."

A tear trickled from Cindy's eye, and she said, "It must be very sad when your best friend forgets you."

Tommy agreed. "It is. I can attest to that. But that's the way humans are."

"Miss Grace," asked Cindy, as if to change the subject, "do you think we could look for Sabrina now?"

But Susie jumped in, "I know where she is. Follow me."

"The 'Christmas Dolls,' " Tommy explained, "always have a little party on Christmas Eve."

As the four of them went through the curtained door that led to the rear of the shop, they quickly discovered Bunny, Annie, and Sabrina sitting at a little table, in a scene reminiscent of *Alice in Wonderland.* But Cindy immediately knew they were not having a tea party.

She could smell the cinnamon and knew hot Christmas cider was being served.

"Sabrina," said Miss Grace, "there's someone here to see you."

"There is?" said the surprised little doll. "How lovely. I wonder who it could be?"

At that, Cindy who had followed Miss Grace into the room, came forward out of the shadows. Sabrina hesitated for just an instant, then she smiled and excitedly said, "Cindy? .... it's Cindy, everybody!"

"Yes, dear," said Miss Grace.

And then, like a small child who had just received a much-desired present from Santa, Sabrina said, "What a lovely Christmas present! Thank you, Miss Grace." Then, with childlike enthusiasm, she asked, "Did you find her at a yard sale, too?"

Miss Grace smiled gently and replied, "No, Sabrina. She came looking for you. She asked me if I knew where you were."

Sabrina studied her best friend, and said, "You've gotten so much taller."

"Yes, I suppose I have," replied Cindy.

Cindy paused for just an instant. Then, she reached down and picked up the doll, just as she had done many, many times before when she was a small child.

"You don't know how many times I thought about you, Sabrina," said Cindy.

"I've missed you, too," the doll replied softly.

"Yes," said Bunny, "she was just talking about you."

"She told us," said Annie, "about the night you first met, almost twenty years ago tonight."

Then, turning to the older woman, Cindy asked, "Miss Grace, why are all the dolls and teddies talking? When I was a child, none of my dolls could talk, except maybe Sabrina."

Miss Grace smiled kindly, and answered, "All these in my shop were the best-loved toy of some child."

"I was Erin's," Bunny explained.

"Who is Erin?" Cindy inquired.

"She was my little girl."

Not to be outdone, Annie interjected, "I had a little girl named Erin, too."

"My Erin's grandmother," continued Bunny, "found me in a little flower shop in Osage, Iowa just after Erin was born. A month later on Christmas Eve, we met for the first time. I liked her right away, but at first, she didn't have much to do with me. Then one day, after she started crawling, she grabbed me by an ear. We went everywhere together for the next seven years."

"My Erin," said Annie wistfully, "only played with me for about two years. Her Erin was a much better friend."

"Even after Erin went into first grade," said the little lavender rabbit, "she used to take me to school. Sometimes she'd leave me in the car, but other times, she'd smuggle me into class in her book bag or lunch box. My favorite class was math. Once, she put me in her coat, and I fell out. I almost lost her that time, but a little boy saw me drop out. He picked me up, ran after her, and gave me back. I think his name was James."

"How," asked Cindy, "did you come to be here?"

"One day," answered Bunny, "at the beginning of second grade, she took me to school in her lunch box, and a boy stole it. He took it home, and when his mother found it, she put both the box and me into a garage sale."

"You should have seen her the first day she came here," said Tommy.

"We could all tell," said Susie Bear, "that she was the most-favorite stuffed animal of all."

"At first," said Tommy, "we all felt sorry for her. She was bare from her ears to her tail...."

"She still had both of her eyes," said Sabrina, "but her nose was gone, and she had been stitched up many times."

"All four of her legs and both of her ears had been sewn back on more than once," explained Miss Grace.

"Erin's mom did that," said Bunny, "I didn't mind the stitches, but I never liked the baths in the washing machine."

"Miss Grace," asked Cindy softly, "could I take Sabrina home? I'll buy her back from you if you like."

Miss Grace gently took Cindy's hand, and said, "Of course you may take her. You'll always belong to each other. But you must promise me that you'll never throw her out again. And more than that, you must never let a doll collector have her."

"I promise," pledged Cindy. "Oh, I promise."

Sabrina looked up at Miss Grace, and said, "I want to go, too." Then she turned to Cindy, and with a small tear in the corner of her eye said, "But I don't think I'll be able to talk with you once we leave here."

But before Cindy could question Sabrina about her misgivings, the small brass bell over the front door tingled, announcing that an uninvited guest had entered the shop. The dolls and stuffed animals froze. The sound of the small bell had awakened Furf, who stretched, and then gave the visitor an in-depth sniff-over.

"Hello?" called the intruder.

Miss Grace and Cindy passed through the curtain to meet the stranger who awaited them in the front room of the shop. Standing near the front door, they saw a woman all in black. In the soft dim light of the Tiffany lamp, she looked almost like a witch.

"Can I help you?" asked Miss Grace. And then turning to Furf, who was still sniffing, Miss Grace said "Down!" Furf obeyed and laid down directly in front of the door and resumed his nap.

"I've stopped by many times," said the woman in black, "but this is the first time I have ever found your shop open."

"To be honest," said Miss Grace, "I'm not really open. I was just showing this young lady a doll."

"How lovely," said the visitor. "That's why I'm here, too. I collect dolls."

"Do you have many?" asked Cindy.

"Yes, my dear," said the gnarled old woman. "I've been collecting dolls for many years. My name is Vendetta Cage."

And then, directing her question to Miss Grace, she asked, "Are you a collector, too?"

"Not exactly," said Miss Grace.

"Could I see," asked Ms. Cage, "some of your pieces?"

Miss Grace replied politely, but without a hint of enthusiasm, "I suppose so." But, she cautioned, "you should know that my dolls and animals are not for sale."

With that, Miss Grace excused herself and went to the room behind the curtain. A few moments later, she returned with Sabrina and Susie.

When Ms. Cage saw them, her eyes lit up, and she exclaimed, "They're lovely! I love antique dolls! Are you sure you won't part with them?"

"What," interjected Cindy, "do you do with the dolls you collect?"

With the great pride of a true collector, Ms. Cage replied, "I store them very carefully in plastic boxes, and keep them on shelves until I can resell them at a reasonable profit. Doll collecting has become a very lucrative business." Then, turning to Miss Grace, she said, "I especially like the ballerina. I'll offer you one hundred dollars

for her." Miss Grace politely thanked her but declined. But Ms. Cage, persisted, "Would you consider one hundred and fifty?" Miss Grace then reiterated, "My dolls are not for sale."

Hearing, but still not believing, the woman in black said, with slight agitation in her voice, "I can't offer you a nickel more than two hundred, or I won't be able to make a profit."

And then, for the first time, Miss Grace's voice betrayed a slight hint of annoyance. "You don't understand. My dolls are simply not for sale."

"I don't believe that," snapped Ms. Cage, clearly frustrated. "Everyone has her price."

Ms. Cage turned as if to leave. But instead of going to the door, she removed a small vial from her purse, which contained a green, magical powder capable of putting humans to sleep and making them forget the very existence of the person using it. Then, emptying a small amount into her hand, she threw it into the eyes of Miss Grace and Cindy, cackled a witch's cackle, and uttered the magic incantation.

"Master, hear a witch's cries.... Blind all foolish human eyes...."

At once, Miss Grace and Cindy fell into a deep sleep. Ms. Cage threw her cape over Sabrina and started to kidnap—or perhaps "doll-nap"—her from the little store.

But as Ms. Cage approached the front door, she found Furf directly in her way, sound asleep, blocking the exit.

"Out of the way, you stupid beast!"

Her shrill command woke Furf, but rather than getting out of the way, the dog got up and, again, began sniffing the old woman. Perhaps, suspecting that something was wrong, Furf put his paws up on her chest, as if to get a closer sniff. "Down, you stupid mutt!"

Furf obeyed, but continued his investigation. And then, perhaps for reasons only a dog can explain, after growling a polite warning, Furf laid down directly in front of the door once again.

Frustrated, and becoming quite angry, Ms. Cage menaced Furf, "Out of the way you worthless fur-ball or I'll change you into a mouse — a sneaky, squeaky mouse! How would you like that, you stupid beast? Instead of a nice home, you'll live in a messy little nest! Nobody will ever pet you again. Your mistress will never again rub your nose. To feel her touch, you'll have to run up her dresses." Then quite pleased with herself, she cackled, "Hee, hee, hee, hee, hee!"

But then, it dawned on her that hers was the nearest dress! "On the other hand, you might run up mine!" Quickly, she changed her mind. "Oops! Not such a good idea!"

It took only a second or so for the old crone to conjure up something even worse.

"I know! Yes, yes, yes! I'll change you into a louse—a wriggling, niggling louse! You'll never see light. You'll burrow and bite! Ha, ha, ha!" But once again, she paused, realizing that she would be the little louse's easiest target. "But then, what if you bite me? After, all, we are in rather close proximity." Quickly she reasoned, "This is a lousy idea."

But old witches don't give up easily. And just then, one more idea flashed into her mind. "I could turn you into a snake—a slithery, leathery snake. Nobody pets snakes." But once more, a complication reared its ugly head. "Then again, I'm afraid of snakes. I'd cower and run if you stuck out your tongue."

Finally, in a moment of pure desperation, Ms. Cage got her most brilliant idea.

"I've got it. I'll turn you into a stuffed toy! Stuffed toys can't bite. Stuffed toys can't hiss. Stuffed toys can only sit dumbly, like this!"

Entirely pleased with herself, Ms. Cage struck a stuffed animal pose. Then for reasons understood only by a canine mind, Furf got to his feet, and once again moved around behind the old witch, sniffing all the while.

Perhaps it was the animus in her tone, because this time, this always friendly dog proceeded to take one big chomp out of her fanny. This act was wildly out of Furf's character, but he didn't let go!

Ms. Cage's next move was quite predictable. She screamed out in pain. "Ouch! Ouch! That hurts! Ouch! Let go!"

Tears came to her eyes, and she said, "You beast, do you know the horrible thing you've done? You've spoiled an old witch's Christmas-time fun!"

Then, becoming increasingly angry, she growled, "I warn you. I'm going to count to three, and then change you into a salamander! One! Two!..."

However once again, she hesitated, as she realized her predicament. "But then again.... since we're so firmly attached... I can't risk changing you into a newt, as I might find myself sharing your suit."

But Furf's teeth (still in her fanny!!) were causing her more than a little discomfort. "Oh! Your teeth are hurting me so! If you'll be kind enough to let me go, I promise I'll do nothing naughty. Just get your fangs out... this isn't funny!"

But Furf didn't let go. Finally, realizing that all was lost, Ms. Cage pleaded, "All right. All right, you can keep the stupid doll!"

As Ms. Cage released Sabrina and allowed the little doll to fall to the floor, Furf released his grip on the witch's behind. Then, having no desire to allow Furf to reattach himself to her backside, the old shrew bolted for the door, and as she did, Furf woofed triumphantly—well, as triumphantly as a dog could, with a piece of Ms. Cage's skirt still dangling from one of his teeth.

As she yanked open the door, Ms. Cage, not to be outdone, turned back to Furf and pointed a menacing gnarled finger at him and warned, "I'll deal with you later."

Furf, looked her straight in the eye, and once again let out a muffled woof.

But the old woman was not inclined to allow any dog to have the last word. From what she judged to be a safe distance, she snarled, "Stupid dog. Now I know why witches only keep cats!"

Furf, with a grim determination, merely repeated himself, "Woof!"

But now, with the pain somewhat abating, Ms. Cage once again found her courage, "Someday, I'll get you for this!"

Furf, as dogs do, now realized that the old woman meant him no good, and he replied with a long, low growl, "Grrrrrr!"

This caused his adversary to pause. "...But I think I'll wait until after Christmas."

Not mollified in the least, Furf's growl dropped into an even lower register, "GRRRRRR!" It was clear he meant serious business.

Ms. Cage understood the full implication of what Furf was saying, and commenced full retreat, muttering as she went, "Yes, after Christmas... next year!"

Then, having exerted himself far beyond his normal daily routine, Furf plopped down and promptly resumed his nap.

Perhaps it was Furf's snoring that woke Miss Grace and Cindy, or maybe the witch's magic lasted only briefly, but almost immediately, the two women awoke. And when they did, they remembered nothing of their encounter with Ms. Cage, but resumed the conversation that they had been having, as if there had been no interruption.

Cindy turned to Miss Grace and said, "Thank you. Thank you, very much."

Miss Grace smiled. "My only desire has ever been to reunite these toys with the children who loved them."

Then, the two women turned and walked into the back room, taking Sabrina and Susie with them to join the rest of the dolls. As they stood there, for a brief moment, Cindy asked, "Miss Grace, a few minutes ago, Sabrina said she might not be able to talk with me once we left this shop. Why not?"

"Because," said Miss Grace, "you're no longer a child, my dear. And adults don't ever love their dolls and need them the way they did when they were little."

Susie explained, "We learned to talk to you then because you always talked to us. You told us all your secrets and why you were happy or sad. You made us your best friends."

"We talked to you," said Annie, "as long as you let us be your best friends."

"But then," asked Cindy, "why are you talking to me now?"

"I don't know for sure," said Annie hesitantly, "Perhaps because Christmas Eve is the night when God gave all his children his own very special gift, and perhaps, because when so many favorite toys are gathered together, there is the same love in this room that you knew when you were little."

"Are you sure," Cindy asked Sabrina, "that you still want to come with me... even if you can't talk to me? Even if I don't spend as much time with you as I did when I was a child?"

"Yes," said Sabrina, without hesitation.

"Why?" asked Cindy.

"Because," said the little ballerina, "once a doll becomes your best friend, we are your best friend forever."

With that, Cindy gathered Sabrina in her arms. Miss Grace gave her a small blanket, and Cindy wrapped the doll up, just as she had done many years ago, before taking her out into the night.

As she opened the front door of the store, she turned back and smiled at the older lady, and said, "Thank you very much. Merry Christmas, Miss Grace."

Miss Grace only smiled.

THE END

Lightning Source UK Ltd.
Milton Keynes UK
UKHW051158131121
393861UK00003B/173